Grizzly Bear Rock

Written by Lesley Sims

Illustrated by Andrew Rowland

How this book works

The story of **Grizzly Bear Rock** has been written for you to read with your child. You take turns to read:

You read these words.

Sal's dream is to be in a rock band.

"I can hum, I can sing. Let me be in!"

5

Your child reads these words.

You don't have to finish the story in one session. If your child is getting tired, put a marker in the page and come back to it later.

You can find out more about helping your child with this book, and with reading in general, on pages 30-31.

2

Grizzly Bear Rock

Turn the page to start the story.

Sal's dream is to be
in a rock band.

"I can hum,
I can sing.
Let me be in!"

5

Now Sal is a star
on the dance floor.

"I can kick,
I can hop.

I can roll,
I can rock."

Sal leaps up on stage with a flourish.

But Sal cannot sing.

It is such a din.

The others all roar,
"Sal, please stop it!"

Sal is so sad.
Can she be that bad?

She sobs and she wails
and she whimpers.

"If I cannot sing,
I cannot be in."

But Sammy on drums has been thinking.

"Sal, bang on a can,

and bash on a pan."

15

"Sal, bang on a can,

and bash on a pan."

15

Sam's plan is a hit. Sal has rhythm!

"Sal, ring on a bell,

and the song
will go well."

The Grizzlies all smile and say,
"Join us!"

"Sal, bang on a gong."

Let US sing the song.

And now all the Grizzlies
are happy.

21

Puzzle 1

Look at the pictures together
and try retelling the story.

1.

2.

3.

4.

5.

6.

You might like to talk about being in a band. Which instrument would you like to play?

Puzzle 2

Match the speech bubbles to the pictures.

Puzzle 3

Look at the picture and read the words below. Which four things are in the picture?

- a bell
- a can
- a fish
- a gong

- a king
- a pan
- a shell
- a ship

Answers to puzzles

Puzzle 1

Use this puzzle to check that your child has understood the story, and have fun discussing music, bands and instruments.

If your child isn't sure what to say, try asking leading questions such as, "Who's this? What are they doing now?" (Of course, there is more than one possible answer.)

Puzzle 2

1. Ring on a bell. – D
2. I can roll, I can rock. – C
3. Bang on a gong. – A
4. It is such a din. – B

Puzzle 3

a bell

a pan

a gong

a can

Guidance notes

Usborne Very First Reading is a series of
books, specially developed for children who are
learning to read. In the early books in the series,
you and your child take turns to read, and
your child steadily builds the knowledge and
confidence to read alone.

The words for your child to read in **Grizzly
Bear Rock** introduce these letter-combinations:

It's important for your child to recognize these
combinations and their sounds, not just read the
letters individually. Be aware that this represents
a more challenging stage in their reading, too.
Later books in the series gradually introduce more
letter-combinations and spelling patterns, while
reinforcing the ones your child already knows.

You'll find lots more information about the
structure of the series, advice on helping your
child with reading, extra practice activities and
games on the Very First Reading website,[*]
www.usborne.com/veryfirstreading

[*]US readers go to **www.veryfirstreading.com**

Some questions and answers

- **Why do I need to read with my child?**
  Sharing stories and taking turns makes reading an enjoyable and fun activity for children. It also helps them to develop confidence and reading stamina, and to take part in an exciting story using very few words.

- **When is a good time to read?**
  Choose a time when you are both relaxed, but not too tired, and there are no distractions. Only read for as long as your child wants to – you can always try again another day.

- **What if my child gets stuck?**
  Don't simply read the problem word yourself, but prompt your child and try to find the right answer together. Similarly, if your child makes a mistake, go back and look at the word together. Don't forget to give plenty of praise and encouragement.

- **We've finished, now what do we do?**
  It's a good idea to read the story several times to give your child more practice and confidence. Then you can try reading **The Magic Ring** at the same level or, when your child is ready, go on to Book 6 in the series.

Edited by Jenny Tyler and Mairi Mackinnon
Designed by Russell Punter

The Grizzlies

— now with Sal!

First published in 2010 by Usborne Publishing Ltd., Usborne House,
83-85 Saffron Hill, London EC1N 8RT, England. www.usborne.com
Copyright © 2010 Usborne Publishing Ltd.

USBORNE VERY FIRST READING

There are twenty-four titles in the **Usborne Very First Reading** series, which has been specially developed to help children learn to read.

To find out more about the structure of the series, go to **www.usborne.com/veryfirstreading**